Try This!

Monica Hughes
Photographs by Lindsay Edwards

Contents

How to Make a Balloon Stick to a Wall

You will need:

 a balloon

 your sweater

1 Blow up the balloon.

2 Tie the end of the balloon.

3 Rub the balloon on your sweater.

4 Put the balloon against a wall.

Does it stick?

How to Make a Telephone

You will need:

 two plastic cups

 a long piece of string

 a pencil

 a friend

1 Make a hole in each cup.*

Like this!

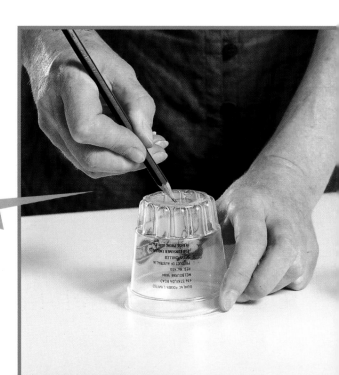

* Have an adult help you.

2 Put the string through the holes.

3 Tie knots.

Like this!

4 Pull the string tight. Speak into one end.

Can your friend hear you?

How to Make a Flower Change Color

You will need:

 a fresh, white flower

 a plastic cup of water

 food coloring

 scissors

1 Put coloring into the water.

This much: 🞄🞄

2 Cut the stem.

Like this!

3 Put the flower in the cup.

4 Leave it in a warm place for a day.

What color is the flower?

How to Make a Volcano

You will need:

 a small, plastic bottle

 clay

 a plastic mat

 baking soda

 red food coloring

 vinegar

1 Put lots of baking soda in the bottle.

This much

2 Add some food coloring.

This much: 🌢🌢🌢

3 Make a shape like a volcano.

Like this!

4 Pour some vinegar into the bottle.

Like this!

What happens?
Add more vinegar and see what happens now.

How to Make a Kaleidoscope

You will need:

 three mirrors

 sticky tape

 waxed paper

 scissors

 shiny paper

 rubber bands

1 Tape the mirrors like this.

2 Cover one end with waxed paper.

3 Put a rubber band around the end.

4 Tear up the shiny paper and drop it in.

Like this!

5 Cover the top with waxed paper and put a rubber band around it.

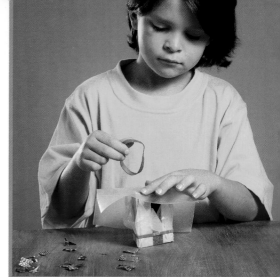

6 Hold your kaleidoscope up to the light. Look through it and shake it.

What can you see?

Try This, Too!

a bottle

vinegar

baking soda

balloon

1 water

vinegar

2 teaspoon

a tissue

3

4 balloon

What happens to the balloon?

Index